Annie and Snowball and the Surprise Day

The Eleventh Book of Their Adventures

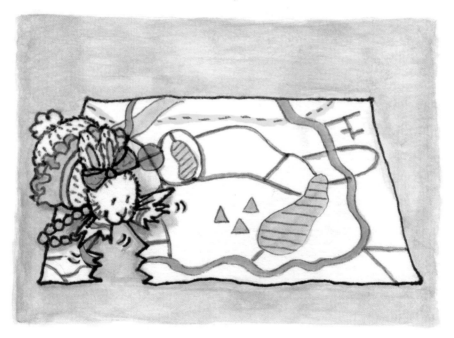

Cynthia Rylant

Illustrated by Suçie Stevenson

READY-TO-READ

SIMON SPOTLIGHT

New York   London   Toronto   Sydney   New Delhi

For Alexandra Penfold —S. S.

SIMON SPOTLIGHT

An imprint of Simon & Schuster Children's Publishing Division
1230 Avenue of the Americas, New York, New York 10020
Text copyright © 2012 by Cynthia Rylant
Illustrations copyright © 2012 by Suçie Stevenson
All rights reserved, including the right of reproduction in whole or in part in any form.
SIMON SPOTLIGHT, READY-TO-READ, and colophon are
registered trademarks of Simon & Schuster, Inc.
For information about special discounts for bulk purchases, please contact
Simon & Schuster Special Sales at 1-866-506-1949 or business@simonandschuster.com.
The Simon & Schuster Speakers Bureau can bring authors to your live event. For more
information or to book an event contact the Simon & Schuster Speakers Bureau at
1-866-248-3049 or visit our website at www.simonspeakers.com.
Designed by Tom Daly
The text of this book was set in Goudy Old Style.
The illustrations for this book were rendered in pen-and-ink and watercolor.
Manufactured in China 0713 SCP
This Simon Spotlight edition March 2012
2 4 6 8 10 9 7 5 3
Library of Congress Cataloging-in-Publication Data
Rylant, Cynthia.
Annie and Snowball and the surprise day : the eleventh book of their adventures /
Cynthia Rylant ; illustrated by Suçie Stevenson.
p. cm. — (Ready-to-read)
Summary: Annie goes on a surprise road trip with her dad and her pet bunny, Snowball.
ISBN 978-1-4169-3944-3 (hardcover : alk. paper)
ISBN 978-1-4424-5101-8 (eBook)
[1. Automobile travel—Fiction. 2. Rabbits—Fiction.] I. Stevenson, Suçie, ill. II. Title.
PZ7.R982Ansu 2012
[E]—dc23
2011018198

Contents

4

Let's Go!

It was a lovely summer day.
Birds sang, flowers bloomed,
children played.

Annie was playing with her pet bunny,
Snowball, in the backyard.

They were playing dress up.
Annie loved playing dress up.

6

Annie's dad called to her.
"Annie!" he said. "I have a surprise."

A surprise?
Annie *loved* surprises.

So did Snowball.

Snowball loved *crunchy* surprises.

9

Annie and Snowball
went inside the house.
Annie's dad was in the kitchen
holding three things:
a map, pink sunglasses,
and a picnic basket.

He put on the pink sunglasses.
"Oops!" said Annie's dad.
"These must be for you."
Annie smiled and took the sunglasses.

"Are we taking a trip?" she asked.
"We are taking a day trip,"
said Annie's dad.
"We are going to be day-trippers."
"Yay!" said Annie.

"Grab Snowball," said Annie's dad,
"and let's go!"

The Map

Annie and Snowball and Annie's dad
hopped in the car.
"Where are we going?" asked Annie.
"I don't know," said Annie's dad.
"Let's pick a road and follow it."

"Okay!" said Annie. She opened the map.

"Which road?" she asked.

"You choose," said Annie's dad.

"Here's where we are."

He pointed to a circle

he had drawn on the map.

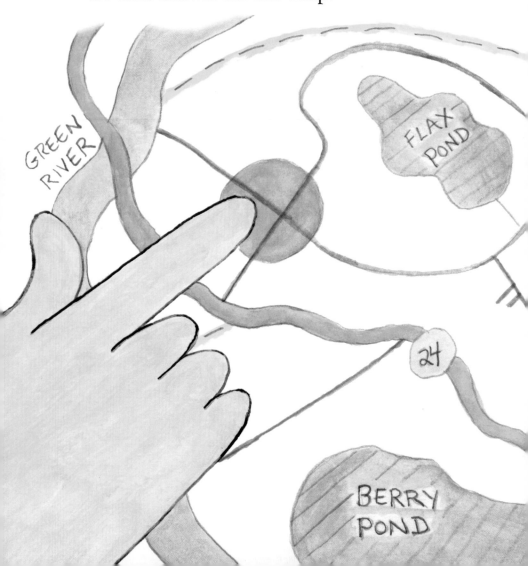

Annie studied the map.

"Hmmm," she said, studying.

Snowball tried to curl up on the map.
Annie laughed.

"Snowball likes *this* road," Annie said.

"She's sniffing it!"

"What number is the road?"
asked Annie's dad.

"24," said Annie.

"Highway 24, here we come!"
said Annie's dad.

He put on his sunglasses.
Annie put on hers.
Snowball jumped into her car box.

And away they went!

Highway 24

It wasn't long before they were
on Highway 24.
"It's a country road," said Annie's dad.
"Good pick."
"Yes," said Annie.
"Snowball did a good job."
"She did a good job with her sniffer,"
said Annie's dad.

They drove along Highway 24.
They rolled the windows down.

They played the radio.

They waved at people on tractors.

They waved at people on bikes.

They stopped at a stand and bought
strawberries and blueberries
and a cabbage for Snowball.

26

They stopped at a bridge and
threw stones in the water.

Then they found a shady rest stop.

"Time to eat!" said Annie's dad.

He opened the picnic basket.

"Surprise!" he said.

Inside the basket
was a beautiful carrot cake—
with a real carrot on top!

"Wow," said Annie. "Thanks, dad."

Annie and her dad had a lovely snack
of strawberries, blueberries, and cake.
And Snowball had a perfect salad!

Annie fed some little birds
bits of her cake.
And her dad left a big strawberry
under a tree in case a turtle stopped by.
Then they hopped in the car for home.

Back Home

When Annie got home later,
she went next door
to tell her cousin Henry about her day.

Henry and his big dog, Mudge,
were reading comic books and drooling.
(Only one of them was drooling.)

34

Annie told Henry
about being a day-tripper.
"Great!" said Henry.

"I saved some cake for you,"
said Annie.
"Thanks!" said Henry.

"And I brought Mudge a stick,"
said Annie.
"Wow," said Henry. "Good stick."

Mudge thought so too.
He bit it right in half!

When Annie and Snowball
went back home,
Annie's dad was looking
at the road map again.

"May we take another day-trip
sometime?" Annie asked.
"Sure," said her dad.
"Which road shall we take?"
asked Annie.

Her dad looked at Snowball.
"Only the nose knows!" he said.
Annie smiled a big smile
and gave her dad a hug.